CH

SPOTLIGHT ON
CIVIC COURAGE
HEROES OF CONSCIENCE™

SOPHIE SCHOLL

STUDENT RESISTER AND ANTI-NAZI POLITICAL ACTIVIST

Michelle McIlroy

Rosen
YA™

New York

Published in 2018 by The Rosen Publishing Group, Inc.
29 East 21st Street, New York, NY 10010

Library of Congress Cataloging-in-Publication Data

Names: McIlroy, Michelle, author.
Title: Sophie Scholl : student resister and anti-Nazi political activist / Michelle McIlroy.
Description: New York : Rosen Publishing, [2018] | Series: Spotlight on civic courage : heroes of conscience | Includes bibliographical references and index. | Audience: Grades 5–10.
Identifiers: LCCN 2017013814| ISBN 9781538381106 (library bound) | ISBN 9781538381076 (pbk.) | ISBN 9781538381083 (6 pack)
Subjects: LCSH: Scholl, Sophie, 1921–1943—Juvenile literature. | Weisse Rose (Resistance group)—Juvenile literature. | Anti-Nazi movement—Juvenile literature. | Women political activists—Germany—Biography—Juvenile literature. | World War, 1939–1945—Germany—Juvenile literature.
Classification: LCC DD256.3.S337 M36 2018 | DDC 943.086/4092 [B] —dc23
LC record available at https://lccn.loc.gov/2017013814

Manufactured in the United States of America

On the cover: Sophie Scholl's courageous resistance to the Nazi regime is still remembered and admired today. The background photo, dated 1938, shows German children, much like Scholl, who were taught to salute Adolf Hitler.

CONTENTS

ON TRIAL BY THE HANGING JUDGE

Sophie Scholl, her brother Hans, and a friend were on trial on February 22, 1943. She was serene, despite facing a room filled with Nazi supporters, who were invited to the court to witness the proceedings. Roland Freisler, the judge conducting this trial, was known as the hanging judge. He used the court to support the Nazi Party by seeing that accused criminals were punished harshly.

Freisler raged and hollered. He yelled and screeched, accusing the three students of high treason, a crime punishable by death. There was no room to question their guilt. Sophie Scholl, her brother, and their friend Christoph Probst had already confessed to these crimes, and their fate was already sealed. Despite his fury, Scholl was confident in her choices and remained calm. By the end of the day, the punishment for treason would be carried out, and Sophie Scholl would give her life for her beliefs at the young age of twenty-one.

Sophie Scholl faced a room filled with Nazi leaders and sympathizers with calm and dignity. Her confidence in her choices was evident even to the lead investigator in her trial.

What Kind of Family Would Raise a Traitor?

Sophie was born on May 9, 1921, in Forchtenberg am Kocher, Germany, the youngest girl of six children. One child died as an infant. When she was born, Germany was a new democracy that faced economic and political unrest. Her parents, Robert and Magdalene Scholl, raised the children to think for themselves and allowed intense discussions about reading, art, and philosophy at home. Sophie's father once said, "What I want most of all is that you live in uprightness and freedom of spirit, no matter how difficult that may be." Her parents maintained friendships with Jewish and artist neighbors even after the Nazi takeover, demonstrating the values of courage and justice they had taught their children. The encouragement to think independently in a

Julia Jentsch, an actress who played the role of Sophie Scholl, pauses in front of Scholl's statue. Scholl is known for her courageous choices and sacrifice during the violent years of Nazi rule of Germany.

Nazi-influenced society gave Sophie and her brother the foundation to later stand up for what was right, even if that meant an enormous personal sacrifice.

Independent Thinking in a Strict German School

Even during the days of the democratic Weimar Republic, German schools mostly focused on teaching children to be disciplined and obedient citizens. There was not much emphasis on critical, independent thinking. Students were even caned, which meant their hands were hit with sticks as a means of discipline. On one occasion, Sophie was hit because she spoke out in disagreement with her teacher. A girl was not allowed to express such strong opinions in school. Girls were expected to learn behavior appropriate for futures as wives who were submissive and subdued.

Even after being punished this way, Sophie kept her fierce independence. In class, the location of a student's seat determined the student's rank. Sophie's sister Elisabeth was demoted by one seat on her birthday, and Sophie angrily demanded that the teacher allow her sister to return to the original seat. Surprisingly, her teacher allowed it. Sophie's sense of justice was clear from a young age.

Scholl demonstrated independence and a clear sense of justice. Today, her actions are honored on a postage stamp (opposite Nobel Peace Prize winner Bertha von Suttner).

Rise of Hitler and Nazi Nationalism in Germany

Sophie was twelve years old when Adolf Hitler rose to power and Nazi nationalism gripped Germany. Germany was in a time of deep unrest and financial struggles, having lost World War I and territory. In 1929, when the Great Depression struck the United States, Germany and other parts of Europe suffered, too. Many people in Germany believed that Hitler and the National Socialist Party could solve their national problems. Hitler spoke with energy and gave the people hope that Germany would become a strong nation again. Adolf Hitler used the radio as a way for ordinary people to hear his message and feel connected to him, giving him power and influence over the masses. Sophie, Hans, and her sister Inge all listened to these promises and believed that Germany would flourish under Adolf Hitler's control. Their parents expressed doubt in this, but Adolf Hitler and his followers were persuasive speakers with influence over Germany's youth.

Adolf Hitler roused Germany into a feverish nationalism. Ruling the National Socialist Party, he gained notoriety through speeches and suppressed his doubters.

PRIDE OF HITLER

The Hitler Youth was an organization that Adolf Hitler used to train children from an early age to support the Third Reich. Sophie's father warned his children against joining any of these youth groups but allowed the children to join if they wanted to. He believed they needed to discover the truth about Nazi nationalism by seeing it for themselves. The programs included camping trips, campfires, and physical training, which appealed to Sophie and her brother Hans, who joined. Members of the Hitler Youth were expected to think as members of the group—not as individuals. Hitler Youth girls could earn badges for sports and showing knowledge of Nazi ideology, nursing, and household training, or learning to become future German housewives. Eventually, Sophie would become a leader in her group, called the League of German Girls. Child leaders were part of Hitler's plan to

The Hitler Youth movement gave Hitler the opportunity to sway the opinions of young Germans. They were involved in parades, marches, camping trips, and other training in preparation for being part of Hitler's regime.

gain control. Child leaders kept children away from adults who might encourage them to question the values the youth groups were teaching them.

SEEDS OF DOUBT

While a member of the League of German Girls, one of Sophie's friends was excluded from joining because of her Jewish heritage. This friend had blonde hair and blue eyes, which were preferred traits in the Nazi regime. Sophie's brown hair and eyes were accepted, though, because Sophie wasn't Jewish. Sophie was disturbed by the anti-Semitism she witnessed in the group. In addition, some of Sophie's favorite books began to disappear from schools and the library. Then, a favorite teacher was removed from class and the SA (or *Sturmabteilungen*, which translates to "storm troopers") spat in his face. He was eventually sent to a concentration camp. It disgusted Sophie that his "crime" was only that he didn't share Nazi political views. Later, Sophie's whole family was arrested when her brother met with a group of anti-Nazi friends while he served mandatory military time. (Arresting an entire family was known as a "clan arrest" and was a common Nazi tactic.) Even though her family was released, her confidence in the regime was gone.

Under Adolf Hitler, German girls experienced unprecedented freedom and attention. Girls were given physical training as well as opportunities to socialize away from the watchful eyes of their parents.

RESISTANCE BY READING

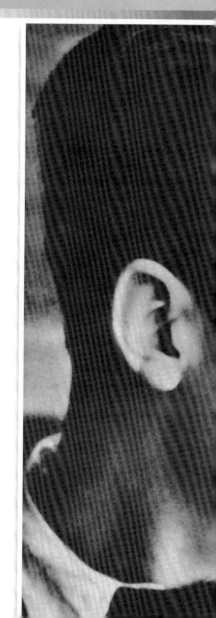

As the Scholl children questioned the Nazi way, they began to separate from the Hitler Youth movement. The Scholl boys joined others who formed a secret group called the dj.1.11, which read banned books, sang banned songs, and enjoyed anti-Nazi friendship. Girls weren't allowed to join the dj.1.11, so the Scholl girls joined other girls in a secret reading circle, too. In this secret reading group, the girls read poetry and books by authors whose work had been banned from libraries and schools and burned. They even printed a small newsletter of forbidden literature. The texts they chose to print were concealed anti-Nazi messages intended to share their political views. While continuing to attend her German League meetings, Sophie recommended a reading by one of the banned authors. She was questioned for suggesting this author, a Jewish poet named Heinrich Heine. Sophie replied saying, "He who doesn't know Heinrich Heine doesn't know German literature." Her resistance had begun.

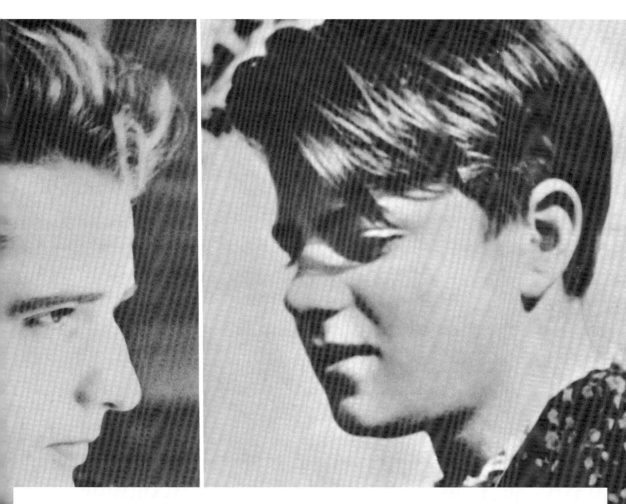

Hans Scholl and Sophie Scholl were close and often discussed politics and philosophy together. The Scholl children were avid readers who believed in independent thinking.

WAITING FOR HER DREAMS

Sophie dreamed of following her brother to university, but her distaste for Nazi nationalism threatened her future. In school, she stopped participating in class discussions. Her principal threatened that she would not pass the Abitur test, which was required to graduate and attend university, if she did not learn to comply with their expectations. His threat worked, and she passed, but she was still not allowed to follow her dreams. All female graduates were required to serve six months in labor service. Hoping to avoid hard labor, Scholl trained as a kindergarten teacher. However, after six months of work, the rules changed, and she found that her service didn't count after all, and she was sent to a labor camp. Then, devastatingly, the rules changed again. Without explanation, the government moved Scholl to still another location for a separate labor service to support the war effort. She was enraged that her dreams of attending university were on hold.

Sophie grew increasingly unhappy with Nazi life as she completed high school. Her dreams of attending university with her brother were put on hold by service in the national labor movement.

ESCAPING WAR IN ART AND NATURE

During these stressful years, Sophie Scholl would sometimes slip away to play music or go for a walk in nature to find tranquility. She wrote in her journals and letters about the peace she found in nature: "I can never look at a limpid stream without at least dangling my feet in it. There is nothing more enticing than a fragrant piece of land … I turn my head; it touches the rough trunk of a nearby apple tree … I press my face to the tree's dusky, warm, bark, and think, 'My homeland.' And I am so inexpressibly grateful." She also loved to draw and enjoyed art the Nazis had deemed unworthy of notice. These escapes—music, nature, and art—helped Scholl in more than one way. Not only did they give her peace, but they also helped maintain her individuality, even as the Nazis made every effort to stamp out all such independence from German society.

A contemplative girl, Sophie Scholl wrote often about the peace she found in nature during the stressful years of the Nazi regime while she completed her labor service.

University at Last!

When May 1942 arrived, Scholl was finally aboard a train bound for Munich and her new life in the university. Her long time in labor service was behind her, and she could finally join her brother. Her family had encouraged her artistic talents and thought she'd pursue a degree in an art institute, but instead she chose philosophy and biology. (She felt that art is not something that you *learn*.) Sophie's brother and close friends warmly welcomed her to Munich. There, they celebrated her twenty-first birthday, complete with a cake, which was something nearly impossible to get in the years of food rations and Nazi control. While in

Genau bec

1 Fachgr.: Vol
   Fachschaft: Vor
       " Kli
       " Zah
       " Pho

4 Fachgr.: Kul
   Fachschaft: German
     Hauptfach: De
   Fachschaft: Geschi
     Hauptfach: Ge
   Fachschaft: Altert
     Hauptfach: lat
   Fachschaft: Neue
     " Kunstg
     " Psycho
     " Philos
     " Musik

Munich, Sophie spent hours with her brother and his group of friends in Hans Scholl's room, enjoying discussions about philosophy, art, books, and politics. It was a rare safe circle of trusted friends who would soon work to change their world.

Finally, Sophie Scholl traveled to Munich and joined her brother at university. She chose biology and philosophy classes, despite her artistic talents. This class card shows classes for one semester.

8 Fachgruppen, die sich in einzelne Fachschaften teilen.

ren zu der Fachschaft, in der Ihr Hauptfach liegt.

2 Fachgr.: **Naturwissenschaft**
Fachschaft: **Chemie**
    „   **Geographie**
    „   **Mathematik und Physik**
    „   **Biologie (Bot. u. Zool.)**

3 Fachgr.: **Wirtschaftswissensch.**
Fachschaft: **Volkswirtschaft**
    „   **Forstwirtschaft**

5 Fachgr.: **Rechtswissenschaft**
keine Unterteilung

6 Fachgr.: **Zeitungswissenschaft**

7 Fachgr.: **Leibeserziehung**

8 Fachgr.: **Tiermedizin**

Welcher **Fachgruppe** und **Fachschaft** gehören Sie an?

Fachgr.: .... *Nat.*

Fachsch.: .... *Biol.*

ü. Kulturwiss.

A Nazi-Purged University

U nder Nazi control, serious changes came to schools and universities. More than 1,200 professors, including Nobel Prize winners, lost their jobs when they were dismissed from teaching. Any books considered un-German were banned and burned. Only literature and curriculum that supported nationalist ideas were allowed to remain. Scholl chose her courses carefully because many courses aimed to further the Nazi political agenda. Disappointingly, the majority of the students also supported Nazi views. In this bleak place, however, she discovered a few rays of hope: Professor Fritz Joachim von Rintelen hid anti-Nazi messages in his Greek history lessons. Philosophy professor Kurt Huber lectured that good would ultimately prevail over evil. But then Professor von Rintelen was fired. His motives had been discovered. A group of students marched in rebellion in front of the chancellor's office after. It gave Sophie Scholl hope to see that there were students willing to speak out for justice in this rigid and threatening climate.

Professor Kurt Huber lectured at the University of Munich and expressed his belief that good would win over evil. He ultimately joined the White Rose resistance group.

DISCOVERING THE WHITE ROSE

Scholl had been in Munich for six weeks when mysterious leaflets began to circulate throughout the university. They called for fellow German scholars and professors to oppose the Nazi regime for a better Germany. When Scholl discovered the first leaflet, she felt a dangerous thrill of excitement. Another student on the campus shared her views on Hitler! She went to discuss this discovery with her brother and discovered materials in his room that made it seem that he was involved with the leaflet campaign. Scholl confronted her brother, but he refused to answer her questions. Simply knowing about such resistance work was

perilous. Eventually, under his sister's relentless pressure, Hans Scholl admitted to his work in writing the leaflets and allowed her to participate. Together with a small group of close friends, the Scholl siblings were called the White Rose, a group actively resisting the "irresponsible clique" they felt their government had become.

Scholl and others are known for their resistance through the production of leaflets. Today, these leaflets are remembered in a bronze memorial embedded in the pavement in front of the University of Munich.

WAR WORK

At the end of the university term, Scholl had to serve mandatory time assisting Germany's war effort in order to qualify for a return to school the following semester. She was sent to a munitions factory. She was miserable there. The work was dull, and many of the women she worked alongside were Nazi fanatics who joyfully supported the war effort. Scholl was at least able to befriend a woman from Russia because the woman had not yet been contaminated by the behavior of her fellow Germans. Germany was at war with Russia, but still she felt a deeper friendship with this woman than the other girls in the factory. She wrote in a letter that the factory turned people into "machines" that worked to care for the "monster" they had created. Her time in this labor service only further motivated Sophie Scholl to resist the Nazis and end the war.

After a successful first term in university, Scholl was forced to assist in the war effort. She was unhappily sent to a munitions factory to do dull and isolating work.

THE HEART OF THE WHITE ROSE

A s soon as Scholl returned to Munich, she resumed her work with the White Rose and was joined by Professor Kurt Huber in their efforts. During the summer, Scholl's father had been arrested for expressing anti-Hitler views while he was at work. His four-month prison sentence may have motivated Sophie Scholl to become the "heart" of the White Rose. She took responsibility for copying leaflets, gathering supplies from a variety of locations in order to avoid suspicion, mailing leaflets, distributing them among members in the university, and managing all of the finances for the group. She even asked

a friend who was serving in the military for Germany's war efforts for a loan of 1,000 reichsmarks, telling him she needed it for a good cause. This level of involvement was extremely dangerous, but she wrote, "One should do only what is true and good and take it for granted that others will do the same."

Sophie Scholl, her brother, and several trusted friends returned to Munich and continued their resistance efforts. Scholl was called the heart of the group, tending to many production needs.

LEAFLETS OF THE WHITE ROSE

Sophie Scholl was the "heart" of the White Rose, supporting others to write. Starting in the spring of 1942 and continuing until February 1943, their resistance letters grew increasingly outspoken against Hitler and his policies. Leaflet 1, written in the spring of 1942, tried to rally Germans to think of a better Germany, without the Nationalist Socialism that was in place. It reminded people that they deserved a better government. Leaflet 2 called on the people to recognize the war crimes that were being committed in the name of their homeland. It addressed the murder of three hundred thousand Jewish people

Nichts ist eines Kulturvo
stand von einer verantwortungsle
Herrscherclique "regieren" zu 1a
ehrliche Deutsche heute seiner F
das Ausmass der Schmach, die übe
wenn einst der Schleier von unse
vollsten und jegliches Mass uner
Tageslicht treten? Wenn das deu
Wesen korrumpiert und zerfallen
im leichtsinnigen Vertrauen auf
Geschichte, das Höchste, das ein
andere Kreatur erhöht, nämlich
heit des Menschen preisgibt, se
Geschichte und es seiner vernünt
die Deutschen so jeder Individu
und feigen Masse geworden sind,

Goethe spricht von den D
dem der Juden und Griechen, abe
es eine seichte, willenlose Her
Innersten gesogen und nun ihres
Unergang hetzen zu lassen. Es s
mehr hat man in langsamer, trüg
jeden einzelnen in ein geistige
darin gefasst lag, wurde er
nur erkannten das drohende Verde
Mahnen war der Tod. Ueber das S
reden sein.

Wenn jeder wartet, bis d
rächenden Nemesis unaufhaltsam
das letze Opfer sinnlos in den
fen sein. Daher muss jeder Einz
der christlichen und abendländi
Stunde sich wehren so viel er k
heit, wider den Faschismus und
Staates. Leistet passiven Wider
Ihr auch seid, verhindert das W
maschine, ehe es zu spät ist, e
sind, gleich Köln, und he die
Hybris eines Untermenschen verb
Volk diejenige Regierung verdie

Aus Friedrich Schiller,

"....Gegen seinen eigenen Zweck
gus ein Meisterstück der Staats-
mächtigen, in sich selbst gegrün
Stärke und Dauerhaftigkeit ware
Ziel hat er so weit erreicht, a
Aber hält man den Zweck, welche
der Menschheit, so muss eine ti
derung treten, die uns der erste
darf das Besten des Staates zum

upon the invasion of Poland and called it a crime against mankind's dignity. The third leaflet was printed in the spring of 1942 as well. In this one, the White Rose begged German citizens to recognize that their greatest threat wasn't Russia and Bolshevism, but the National Socialists.

s e n R o s e .

als sich ohne Wider-
Trieben ergebenen
ht so, dass sich jeder
und wer von uns annt
Kinder kommen wird,
en ist und die grauen-
tenden Verbrechen ans
so in seinem tiefsten
e eine Hand zu regen,
Gesetzmässigkeit der
und das ihn über jede
preisgibt, die Frei-
ifen in das Rad der
ng unterzuordnen, wenn
so sehr zur geistlosen
rdiehen sie den Untergang.

a tragischen Volke, gleich
er den Anschein, als sei
denen das Mark aus dem
bereit sind sich in den
es ist nicht so; viel-
tischer Vergewaltigung
ckt, und crät, als er
ssen bewusst. Wenige
hn für ihr heroisches
enschen wird noch zu

werden die Boten der
ücken, dann wird auch
ttlichen Dämons gewor-
twortung als Mitglied
ost in dieser letzten
er die Geisel der Mensch-
e System des absoluten
s t a n d - wo immer
ateistischen Kriegs-
ädte ein Trümmerhaufen
Volkes irgendwo für die
st nicht, dass ein jedes
t!

so ist sie verwerflich und schädlich, sie mag übrigens noch so durchdacht und in ihrer Art noch so vollkommen sein. Ihre Dauerhaftigkeit selbst gereicht ihr alsdann vielmehr zum Vorwurf, als zum Ruhme - sie ist dann nur ein verlängertes Uebel; je länger sie Bestand hat, umso schädlicher ist sie.
.....Auf Unkosten aller sittlichen Gefühle wurde das politische Verdiens errungen und die Fähigkeit dazu ausgebildet. In Sparta gab es keine eheliche Liebe, keine Mutterliebe, keine kindliche Liebe, keine Freund-schaft - es gab nichts als Bürger, nichts als bürgerliche Tugend.
.....Ein Staatsgesetz machte den Spartanern die Unmenschlichkeit gegen ihre Sklaven zur Pflicht; in diesen unglücklichen Schlachtopfern wurde die Menschheit beschimpft und misshandelt. In dem spartanischen Gesetz-buche selbst wurde der gefährliche Grundsatz gepredigt, Menschen als Mittel und nicht als Zwecke zu betrachten - dadurch wurden die Grundfest des Naturrechtes und der Sittlichkeit gesetzmässig eingerissen.
.....Welch schöneres Schauspiel gibt der rauhe Krieger Cajus Marcius in seinem Lager vor Rom, der Rache und Sieg aufopfert, weil er die Tränen der Mutter nicht fliessen sehen kann!"

"...Der Staat (des Lykurgus) könnte nur unter der einzigen Bedingung fortdauern, wenn der Geist des Volks stillstünde; er könnte sich also nur dadurch erhalten, dass er den höchsten und einzigen Zweck eines Staates verfehlte."

Aus Goethe "Des Epimenides Erwachen", zweiter Aufzug, vierter Auftritt:

Genien

.....
Doch was dem Abgrund kühn entstiegen,
Kann durch ein ehernes Geschick
Den halben Weltkreis übersiegen,
Zum Abgrund muss es doch zurück.
Schon droht ein ungeheures Bangen,
Vergebens wird er widerstehn!
Und alle, die noch an ihn hangen,
Sie müssen mit zu Grunde gehn

Hoffnung

Nun begegn' ich meinen Braven,
Die sich in der Nacht versammelt
Um zu schweigen, nicht zu schlafen,
Und das schöne Wort der Freiheit

The leaflets of the White Rose were initially intended to gain the attention of students and professors of the University of Munich.

g d

e d
de.
bar
h c
nst
ors
an die Stelle der Gewun-
k abgevon e hat. Alles
orden, nur dasjenige
Menst selbst

Freiheit!

Christoph Probst was another member of the White Rose resistance movement. He joined Sophie Scholl and her brother and faced trial with them in the end.

During the summer of 1942, with the printing of the fourth leaflet, the White Rose shifted focus to speak to the religious members of the Lutheran and Catholic churches to act in the resistance. It proclaimed, "We will not keep silent! We are your guilty conscience!" Sophie Scholl and her brother were called to war service after the printing of the fourth leaflet. After six months without new leaflets, the fifth leaflet discussed the war losses Germany had suffered and Hitler's lies about them. Professor Huber wrote the last printed leaflet, number six. This leaflet begged the German people to see the terrible losses war had cost them and how the Nazis had manipulated the German people into being unthinking and unfeeling. Sophie and her brother delivered this leaflet in February 1943, while other copies were mailed across Germany to other cities. Leaflet 7 was never printed for distribution, but a draft was discovered in the room of Christoph Probst. It cost Probst his life.

A Final Visit to Lecture Hall

On Thursday, February 18, 1943, Sophie Scholl and her brother headed to the university lecture hall with more than fifteen hundred leaflets. The siblings planned to carry out a daring resistance action on behalf of the White Rose. They hoped that these heroic actions would weaken the Third Reich and bring about a better Germany. Sophie and her brother began to place the leaflets on shelves, windowsills, and landings all over the lecture hall. On an impulse, she made a fateful choice. She tossed a handful of leaflets over a balcony railing as the lectures were dismissing. The janitor witnessed this, chased them, and grabbed her brother. Instead of running to save herself, Sophie Scholl remained by her brother's side. Within half an hour, the investigation began. The lead investigator believed Sophie must be innocent because she was so calm as they questioned her. But the leaflets were gathered and placed in her briefcase, where they fit perfectly.

On February 18, 1943, Sophie Scholl and her brother distributed leaflets at the university lecture hall, where they were arrested. Sophie Scholl's courage is remembered at a Berlin, Germany, wax museum.

COURAGEOUS MARTYRS

The interrogations of the Scholl siblings lasted for hours. The two were separated during questioning. Robert Mohr, the lead investigator, tried to get Sophie Scholl to plead not guilty. Declaring innocence and blaming her brother could have saved her, but she refused. She told Mohr that she had chosen for herself and that the Nazi way of life was wrong. Soon after, the Scholls were brought to trial under Freisler. Sophie Scholl only interrupted Freisler once to say, "Someone had to make a start. What we said and what we did are what many people are thinking. They just don't dare say it out loud." Mohr saw Scholl in her cell just prior to her execution. He later commented that her obvious faith and courage left him shaken. Just

before her execution, Scholl said, "Will my death matter if because of our actions thousands of people will be awakened and stirred to action?" Sophie Scholl faced death heroically—with the same bravery that had helped her resist the powerful Nazi regime throughout her young life.

Roland Freisler presided over the People's Court and the trial of Sophie Scholl, Hans Scholl, and Christoph Probst in February 1943. He was known throughout Germany as the hanging judge.

BEYOND THE WHITE ROSE

After the executions of Sophie and Hans, the remaining Scholl family members were arrested under the Nazi policy of "clan arrest." Werner Scholl was sent to the war front, where he was killed. The women were released, but Robert Scholl served a two-year forced labor sentence. Other members of the White Rose were arrested and executed for their involvement in the cause. Even so, copies of the leaflets continued to spread through Germany and were smuggled into other countries. When the Allies moved into Germany, tens of thousands of the leaflets were dropped over Germany by aircraft. Despite the heavy toll, the resistance had carried on. Sophie Scholl, her brother, and others resisted the Nazi regime at a time when

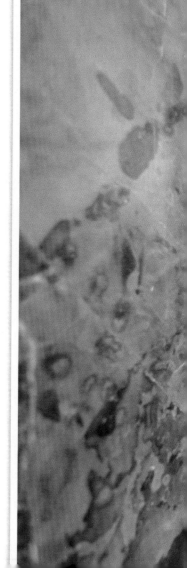

it would have been safer to disregard the terrible things that were happening around them. Today, Germany is a democracy that declares freedom of religion, expression, and dignity for every citizen—the very rights for which Scholl so courageously gave her life.

A statue of Sophie Scholl gazes over the Ludwig Maximilian Lecture Hall at the Munich University, where she is remembered today for her courageous resistance to the Nazi regime.

GLOSSARY

Abitur A test that was given to all German students in order to graduate from high school and qualify for university.

Allies The countries that fought against Germany, Italy, and Japan during World War II.

anti-Semitism Prejudice and hostile behavior or attitudes against Jewish people.

Bolshevism Communist form of government practiced by Russia after 1917.

clique A small group of people with common goals or interests who do not let others join them easily.

concentration camp A place where many targeted people were placed during the time of Adolf Hitler's reign over Germany; where people were forced to provide free labor and where many were eventually executed.

forced labor A form of very hard work for no pay, often used as punishment during the Nazi regime.

Great Depression A time of great economic and political difficulty in the United States and Europe after the 1929 stock market crash.

martyr A person who is killed because of his or her beliefs.

munitions factory A place where military equipment and weapons are produced.

nationalism A sometimes extreme form of patriotism characterized by the belief that one's country is superior to others and should be defended and preserved above all others.

Nazi A member of, or relating to, the National Socialist German Workers' Party, which controlled Germany from 1933 to 1945 under Adolf Hitler.

regime A government, specifically one ruled by a dictator, that values order and control over the freedoms of its citizens.

reichsmark Form of money used by the Third Reich in Germany until 1948.

storm trooper A soldier in a private Nazi army, known for being aggressive and violent. Also known as SA (*Sturmabteilungen*) or Brownshirts.

Third Reich Name given to the period of Nazi rule of Germany (1933–1945).

Weimar Republic Germany's first democratic government, which was developed after World War I as a result of the Treaty of Versailles.

FOR MORE INFORMATION

Anti-Defamation League (ADL)

605 3rd Avenue

New York, NY 10158

(212) 885-7700

Website: http://www.adl.org

Facebook: @anti.defamation.league

Twitter: @ADL_National

Instagram: @adl_national

ADL works to combat hate and encourage responsible citizenship through awareness and activism. With educational resources about the Holocaust and resistance movements, the ADL highlights current events and the need for continued action toward a more tolerant society.

Holocaust Center for Humanity

2045 2nd Avenue

Seattle, WA 98121

(206) 582-3000

Website: https://www.holocaustcenterseattle.org

Facebook: @HCHSeattle

Twitter: @HolocaustCtr

This organization teaches tolerance and citizenship through the lens of the Holocaust. It provides a library of resources, survivors' voices, and other educational materials to enable students to learn Holocaust history and how to apply these lessons to citizenship today.

Illinois Holocaust Museum & Education Center

9603 Woods Drive

Skokie, IL 60077

(847) 967-4800

Website: https://www.ilholocaustmuseum.org

Facebook: @IHMEC

Twitter: @ihmec

Instagram: @ihmec

Their message states, "Take history to heart. Take a stand for humanity." The museum educates students to stand against hatred and honor those who lost their lives during the Holocaust.

Montreal Holocaust Museum

5151 Cote Ste. Catherine Road

Montreal, Quebec, H3W 1M6

Canada

(514) 345-2605

Email: info@museeholocauste.ca

Website: http://museeholocauste.ca/en

Facebook: @Musée-de-lHolocauste-Montréal

Twitter: @MuseeHolocauste

The museum aims to educate students on the political, economic, and historical climate leading up to the Holocaust, using the testimonies of survivors and online opportunities.

Yad Vashem: The World Holocaust Remembrance Center

Har Hazikaron

PO Box 3477

Jerusalem 9103401

Israel

(972) 2 6443400

Email: webmaster@yadvashem.org.il

Website: http://www.yadvashem.org

Facebook: @yadvashem

Twitter: @yadvashem

Instagram: @yadvashem

The Yad Vashem Holocaust Remembrance Center works to be the ultimate global source of Holocaust documentation and research with digital collections from around the world.

WEBSITES

Because of the changing nature of internet links, Rosen Publishing has developed an online list of websites related to the subject of this book. This site is updated regularly. Please use this link to access this list:

http://www.rosenlinks.com/CIVC/Scholl

Byers, Anne. *Courageous Teen Resisters: Primary Sources from the Holocaust*. New York, NY: Enslow Publishing, 2010.

Greek, Joe. *Righteous Gentiles: Non-Jews Who Fought Against Genocide*. New York, NY: Rosen Publishing, 2015.

Levine, Ellen. *Darkness over Denmark: The Danish Resistance and the Rescue of the Jews*. New York, NY: Holiday House, 2000.

Lowery, Zoe. *The Nazi Regime and the Holocaust*. New York, NY: Rosen Publishing, 2017.

Rogow, Sally M. *Faces of Courage: Young Heroes of World War II*. Vancouver, Canada: Granville Island Publishing, 2003.

Rubin, Susan Goldman, and Ela Weissberger. *The Cat with the Yellow Star: Coming of Age in Terezin*. New York, NY: Holiday House, 2006.

Sahgal, Lara, and Toby Axelrod. *Hans and Sophie Scholl*. New York, NY: Rosen Publishing, 2016.

Shuter, Jane. *Resistance to the Nazis*. Chicago, IL: Heinemann Library, 2003.

Steele, Philip. *The Holocaust*. New York, NY: Scholastic, Inc., 2016.

Van Stockum, Hilda. *The Borrowed House*. Bathgate, ND: Bethlehem Books, 2000.

Zullo, Allan, and Mara Bovsun. *Heroes of the Holocaust: True Stories of Rescues by Teens*. New York, NY: Scholastic, Inc., 2005.

BIBLIOGRAPHY

Atwood, Kathryn J. *Women Heroes of World War II*. Chicago, IL: Chicago Review Press, Inc., 2011.

Bartoletti, Susan Campbell. *Hitler Youth: Growing Up in Hitler's Shadow*. New York, NY: Scholastic, 2005.

Dumbach, Annette, and Jud Newborn. *Sophie Scholl and the White Rose*. Oxford, England: Oneworld Publications, 2006.

Freedman, Russell. *We Will Not Be Silent: The White Rose Student Resistance Movement That Defied Adolf Hitler*. New York, NY: Clarion Books, 2016.

Hanser, Richard. *A Noble Treason: The Revolt of the Munich Students Against Hitler*. New York, NY: G. P. Putnam's Sons, 1979.

Lisciotto, Carmelo, and Webb Lisciotto. "The White Rose" Holocaust Research Project. Retrieved January 23, 2017. http://www .holocaustresearchproject.org/revolt/whiterose.html.

Sachs, Ruth Hanna. "The Leaflets." Center for White Rose Studies. Retrieved January 26, 2017. http:www.white-rose-studies.org /The_Leaflets.html.

Scholl, Hans, and Sophie Scholl. *At the Heart of the White Rose: Letters and Diaries of Hans and Sophie Scholl*. Edited by Inge Jens. New York, NY: Harper & Row, 1987.

Trueman, C. N. "Sophie Scholl." The History Learning Site. Retrieved January 23, 2017, historylearningsite.co.uk.

Vinke, Hermann. *The Short Life of Sophie Scholl*. New York, NY: Harper & Row, 1980.

INDEX

ABOUT THE AUTHOR

Michelle McIlroy spent more than a decade working as a fifth-grade teacher in upstate New York. While teaching, she worked to encourage students to engage in critical thinking and analyzing perspectives in reading, particularly with materials pertaining to world events, both historical and current. McIlroy believes that we have a responsibility to discuss tolerance, citizenship, and living courageously for a kinder world with our students. McIlroy feels there is an opportunity for students to engage in these important conversations around reading this book.

PHOTO CREDITS